First Prize

by Lynne Coulter
illustrated by Clive Taylor

Harcourt
SCHOOL PUBLISHERS

Requests for permission to make copies of any part of the work should be addressed to School Permissions and Copyrights, Harcourt, Inc., 6277 Sea Harbor Drive, Orlando, Florida 32887–6777. Fax: 407-345-2418.

Printed in China

ISBN 10: 0-15-351424-8
ISBN 13: 978-0-15-351424-1

Ordering Options
ISBN 10: 0-15-351212-1 (Grade 2 Advanced Collection)
ISBN 13: 978-0-15-351212-4 (Grade 2 Advanced Collection)
ISBN 10: 0-15-358059-3 (package of 5)
ISBN 13: 978-0-15-358059-8 (package of 5)

11 12 13 14 15   0940   15 14 13 12 11 10

Joe was so excited that he ran all the way to the school gate.

"Guess what?" he said to his mom. "At school, we have to read this book and then write a book review. The best book review wins a special prize."

That afternoon, Joe curled up in a cozy chair and read *The Biggest Cake*—a book about a famous chef called Mr. Mack. Joe liked books about real people.

Joe learned that Mr. Mack had baked
the biggest cake in the world to celebrate
his mother's sixtieth birthday. Joe read
until he was finished with the book and
then went to tell his mom about it.

Joe told Mom the entire story about Mr. Mack. He showed her pictures, too.

"Mr. Mack baked a banana cake big enough to feed more than two hundred people," Joe concluded excitedly.

"What an enchanting birthday surprise," said Mom.

"I wonder how Mr. Mack mixed the bananas, flour, sugar, butter, and eggs," said Joe. "He would need a really big mixer and a really huge bowl. I'll bet he needed a really big oven to cook such an enormous cake," Joe continued.

Joe thought that *The Biggest Cake* was the best book he had ever read.

"If only I could meet Mr. Mack," thought Joe. "I would ask him all about the recipe for the huge cake."

Joe sat down to write his book review. When he was finished, he was very pleased with it. He typed it carefully on the computer and turned it in the next day.

Finally, the day came when the winner would be announced. Joe's teacher stood in front of the class. "There are so many good reviews," she said, "but the winner is . . . Anita!"

Joe's face went red with disappointment
because he had thought surely he would
win. He had put so much effort into
writing his review, and he had wanted
to win.

"The first prize is a huge cake made by Mr. Mack," said Joe's teacher. "Mr. Mack himself is here to award the prize!"

Instead of feeling sad about not winning the prize, Joe was thrilled. Now he could ask Mr. Mack all the questions he wanted the answers to.

Joe asked Mr. Mack about the recipe, and they discussed Mr. Mack's book. Joe even got Mr. Mack's autograph.

Anita cut the cake, and everyone said it was the most delicious cake they had ever tasted. Joe thought it was fantastic.

"Are you sorry that you didn't win the prize?" Mr. Mack asked Joe.

"Eating cake with you, Mr. Mack, is the best prize ever!" smiled Joe.

Think Critically

1. Why did Mr. Mack bake the biggest cake in the world?

2. What is a word that means the same thing as *enchanting* does on page 6?

3. Did you think Joe would win first prize? Why or why not?

4. What were the two different settings in the story?

5. When did you first begin to think that Joe was enjoying the book? Read aloud the part that made you think that.

 **Language Arts**

Write a Book Review Write a book review of *First Prize*. Include the title, author, and what you liked or didn't like about the book.

 School-Home Connection Share *First Prize* with a family member. Then talk about your favorite book.